Swimming the Storm

By

Michael Coulombe

Swimming the Storm
by Michael J. Coulombe

Copyright © 2003 by Storm Publications
ISBN # 978-1-890799-40-3

Book production by Storm Publications

Cover design by Armin Torrentos, Jr.

First printing: July 2003
Second printing: March 2008

Storm Publications
PO Box 3168
Burbank, CA 91508-3168
michael.coulombe@gmail.com
www.michaelcoulombe.com

To the little men –
T.J., Matthew,
Christopher, and Majd

TABLE OF CONTENTS

Introduction.. 9

Section 1: Anger

Cinnamon.. 15
Why?.. 18
Why Am I The Enemy?.. 19
You Are No Longer Invited................................... 20
I Don't Want To: I Can't Do It.............................. 21
The Colors Of Love.. 22
I Hate You!... 23
Resentment.. 24
Anger Is Difficult To Eat................................... 25
I Am Anger.. 26
I Had Every Chance To Be Strong............................. 27
Tear.. 28

Section 2: Doubt

Gloomy.. 33
More To Say... 35
I Feel Like I'm Losing...................................... 36
I Don't Want To Cry... 38
Remember Me?.. 40
Need.. 41
I Hear Shakespeare.. 42
Atheist... 43
Amazing... 44
The Path To Hell.. 45
Towards The Finish Line..................................... 46

Section 3: Isolation / Depression

Isolation... 51
Reasonable Doubt... 53
The Edge Of The World....................................... 55
Searching... 56
The Seduction Of Fear.. 57
Missing You.. 58
Sixteen-Year-Old Face... 61
In My Dreams... 63
Swimming The Storm.. 64
One Love.. 66
Dreaming.. 68
Good-Bye.. 70

Section 4: Acceptance / Faith

Almost.. 75
Someone... 77
Speaking To Me.. 78
Winter Wind.. 79
Nature's Bounty... 80
I Belong Here.. 81
I Am The Moon.. 82
A Kiss... 84
Life – A Circle... 85

Rainbow.. 87

Acknowledgements... 91

First the thoughts present themselves, entwined one over another. Cautiously I separate them, laying each away from the others. Gently, I take the strongest one and twist it around my fingers. Next comes a whirlwind of ideas looking for an outlet. Cascading into my open hands the words pour out, that one strand of thought now lost in the overflow. The whirlwind ceases and I close my eyes. Casting away the remaining thoughts, I open my hands to set the words free. They scatter themselves across the page forming a signature beneath the words…

Michael Coulombe and I met when we were twelve and thirteen years old. We had no thoughts for love or romance…only for the allure of what would happen to us "when we grew up." All through high school we racked up frightening telephone bills and spent most of our allowance on postage, since we lived over 60 miles apart and saw each other only once a year.

We were forever writing letters and sending story and play ideas back and forth to one another. We spent our teenage years editing each other's work and learning about different writing styles. We spent hours brainstorming together and developing characters. Even then, Michael expressed his most poignant thoughts through prose and poetry. While we sometimes grew in different directions, we still "grew up" together…always; our romantic hearts were pining for harmony…both with people and with words.

And boy, did we share words! We wrote of our dreams, our aspirations, and (eventually) of love and disappointment. When I read our innocent, carefree poetry of yesteryear, I long for the days when love was new…the butterflies with permanent residence in the pit of your belly, the excitement of "is he going to kiss me," and the clarity of the one who held your hand at school where EVERYONE could see it.

Love was so fresh and so new and it hurt so much more. But it was exciting! And through it all, Michael and I wrote.

I always knew that Michael would be a writer. The words burn inside of him until they are forced out through his pencil. I knew that his love for words would consume him and set him on a literary path. I never doubted that the day when I would see his work published, bound, and at every major bookstore would come. I always knew that autographed copies of everything he ever wrote would grace my bookshelves because I always have had faith in Michael...especially when he doubted himself.

Self-discovery is a long, strenuous path that writing forces you down. In order to have strong ideas, they have to be realistic. And in order to be realistic, one must endure. Michael has endured his share of heartache and has always persevered.

Never do I worry about Michael's career...only for his heart. People are filled with such mindless rage and hatred, that I feared his gentle soul would be bruised and eventually killed.

Michael helped me to better appreciate the differences that he and I had. He helped me to be more aware of the shortcomings that we as a society have...instead of teaching children to embrace unique qualities in people, they are taught to hate those who are not like them. Michael never gave up his personal fight and I have never left his side...armed with my love and faith in him. By standing beside him, I am re-given the gift of his friendship over and over again.

My wedding day was made sweeter by the beautiful song that Michael wrote and sang for my husband and me. Our friendship has prevailed through the meeting, the loving, the leaving, and the being left. We have endured the inevitable times that tested our friendship. What was the survival skill that eased us through? We talked and wrote about all of it...how it made us feel, how we thought others would feel in

10

the same situation. We wrote stories, plays, lyrics, and, of course, poetry.

In this day and age, poetry seems lost-especially in the tragic year we have all endured. Yet to the cherished few, there is poetry in everything...in the collapse of an awesome building; in the majesty of a country's flag in the breeze; in the fracture of a fragile heart; in the blossom of a single dandelion in a sidewalk crack. There are those who can look at the heartbreak and find glory in it.

Michael Coulombe is one of those cherished souls, and I thank him for capturing not only the love and beauty of the world, but the passion and anguish that are an integral part of reality. Journey with him as he takes us through the reality that is his, as well as ours ...be reminded of the world's poetry ...take the thoughts and ideas shared within these pages and twist them around YOUR fingers. Release the words in your heart as you read the words released here. Walk with me as I explore the thoughts and journeys of a true poetic genius.

Ginny Miller
2002

Section 1: Anger

When I am angry I can write, pray, and preach
well, for then my whole temperament is
quickened, my understanding sharpened, and all
mundane vexations and temptations depart.

-- Martin Luther

Cinnamon

The house reeks of cinnamon. Everywhere I turn the faint aroma reminds me of you. It brings to mind those Thanksgivings at your family's house where we made apple pie for dessert. Each slice was savored with the delicious taste of cinnamon. It was so tender and flaky. That apple pie was consistent with each holiday as if it would just always be there – and that made the season so full of warmth and cheer. Now I can't even look at an apple pie, forget about having a slice. The one time I tried after you left tasted like acid on my tongue. Each morsel was rancid; the flavor nothing short of tasteless scraps of stale browned fruit. That apple pie is as *stale* as that memory, as *stale* as our relationship.

I would like to say that those were happier times back then; but it isn't true. Your mother never once stopped complaining. Somehow the pie wasn't warm enough; somehow it had too much cinnamon; somehow I wasn't good enough for you. Somehow that apple pie was my albatross for loving you. It could just never be that we made the pie every year as a family or that since it was made with cinnamon it always tasted perfect. It was just a pie. It was just our love. How was I to be blamed for both?

I don't know how you spent the first years of your life there with your mother. I don't know how the constant nagging never drove you insane. Well actually, the truth is, now that you left, I clearly see the family resemblance.

It all seems so long ago really, like some faded and distant memory, which is clouded by my anger. My anger towards you has been around here so long now that I'm thinking of charging it rent. It's hanging around longer than you ever did. On my good days, which are few in number, I can recall those cold nights when you would drink apple cider by the fireplace and invited me to have some with you. I loved those nights. They were as good to me then as that stick of cinnamon you had in your cider. It was so cozy to have you next to me, to hear the crackling of the fire, to feel the warmth of your breath on one side of my face and that of the fire on the other side. The house smelled so good too. Every night now when I go to sleep and that stench sweeps through the house, I silently close my eyes and I pray you choke on it wherever you are. Even now the bittersweet fragrance in each room makes me want to gag.

Damn, that incessant scent. It's everywhere. Why cinnamon? It haunts the halls at night. It sneaks around the corners to jump out at me. Just when I come through a doorway feeling good, it springs out at me. I hate that. Before you, I enjoyed the smell of cinnamon. Thanks for ruining it for me!

I have mopped the floors, wiped down the counters, and disinfected every inch of this house but the walls bleed that cinnamon crap. They cry cinnamon tears as they mourn your painful absence. Your closet is empty, your side of the bed cold - - I couldn't stand any longer to roll over evening after evening and smell cinnamon remnants of you. I despise sleeping with the memory of you! It's bad enough that you're not here. But now that you're gone, it's getting more sex than you are. I caress your pillow, and keep it lodged behind my back and pretend it's you. At night, when I'm half asleep, I can't tell the difference. I always think of how it used to be when your gentle touch spoke the words you could never say.

The only thing remaining in my life is that gut wrenching smell. You took everything else – like my fucking heart, which you left on the floor to die like some fish out of water gasping for life – why didn't you just throw it back in the water? Or better yet, why didn't you step on it some more extinguishing it of all life? Perhaps dragging my love through the mud wasn't satisfying enough, you should've come back to finish the job. Hell, my love didn't seem to fulfill your insatiable desires; how could I expect anything else to? Now you leave behind this putrid odor of cinnamon as an empty token of your love. Screw you and your cinnamon! I don't want it.

Sometimes I am so foolish and that is so frustrating. Maybe that's my problem. Maybe I expected too much from you. I sure as hell never meant to overload your already sensitive psyche. For crying out loud! You had problems showing love --couldn't you of at least have said it once and mean it: I love you! It's not that hard! It's three simple words. You have a college education; even this simple task falls within your capacity! You act as if these emotions would kill you. The truth is, you broke my heart. What do you have to say for yourself?

I hate you! You have to know that. And that is so easy for me to say too. I'm raw with bitterness after loving you. I will never go down this road again. Mind blowing anger consumes my every thought. I'm constantly torn between that and the awful stench of cinnamon. It's almost its own entity. I hold my breath whenever I enter the house waiting for it to rear its ugly head – just like you did. Perhaps, like you, it's waiting for the right moment to lash out at me the same as you when you condemned me to this existence. Ah cinnamon! Perhaps that smell's hanging on to see if I trust it; to give claim to my heart like I claimed yours. Ha! You didn't stay long enough to claim anything! You have no right to even act like you knew me.

There are even times I hope I see you when I'm out driving. I swear to God, I can make it look like an accident. I want you to hurt as bad as I hurt. I want to torture you slowly and painfully – like smelling cinnamon every day – then you'll know what your memory does to me when I'm forced to go on, against my will, with the imprint of you burned in my mind.

I hope that you think of me with your new partner. When you passionately kiss someone else, I pray you taste my lips and smell my breath laced with the same cinnamon you taught me to love. I want it to disturb your dreams. I hope, really hope, that every time you think of me a little piece of you dies until you fade away to dust; that you agonize over every intimate memory of the life we shared before you turned your back on me. Ah cinnamon; the sweet smell of cinnamon. How do you like cinnamon now?

Why?

Why did you say you loved me if you were scared?
Why did you kiss me passionately if you doubted those
feelings there?
Why was it okay for you to run and hide behind your fears –
    then give me pathetic looks when I released anguish in
my tears?

If this was the best thing you ever had
    and you no longer felt afraid –
and you finally found someone who wouldn't
    let reality stand in the way –
and their passion for love and their zest for life
    could invigorate your soul,
then why let your painful past hasten you away?

Why am I left feeling empty?
    Why do you act like you don't care?
Why does denial consume our apathy
and leave us feeling bare?

Why did I trust you wouldn't hurt me?
    Were your assurances feigning pride?
Your hateful words admonished me every single time I tried.

Is it too late to say, "I love you."?
    Would you believe me if I did?
I have never ever lied to you;
    there was truth in all I said.

And I know these are only questions,
    but they constantly plague my mind.
Was I asking too much for love returned
    and a chance to make it shine?

Why Am I The Enemy?

Why am I the enemy? It was I who held you close.
Why am I the enemy? I know you better than anyone knows.

Why am I the hunted sought after by your rage,
 being force-fed all your angry words like your pet,
locked in a cage?

I loved you like a flower
a precious little gift –
I strove to make you happy;
I saw to every wish.

I listened to your fears and doubts,
    through tear-streaked hiccuped moans,
I clung to every word you said as if they were my own.

You acted as if our souls were one that we could never part-
or like a flower that would wither if ever we were apart.

So then why am I the enemy,
as if my presence means your doom,
and that the very thought of seeing me
keeps us apart in separate rooms?

And if you loved me like you said you did then why push me
away?
Isn't love supposed to keep us together - - not destroy us
every day?

Why am I the enemy left alone, confused, and scared,
when I understand that this is hard for you, when I was
always there?

Why am I left feeling empty as if my love was just denied?
My heart feels like it's been stepped on and abandoned by
you, to die.

At times I want to hate you.
(Sometimes I wish I could.)
But what does it matter anymore?
To you, our love was never good.

You Are No Longer Invited

And you're here, why?
> You are no longer invited.

You know I blame you, right?
You know that I don't need your side of the story, right?
You know that it was *my* friend who came running to cry on
my shoulder because of *you*, right?

I don't want your excuses:
> You are no longer invited!

I always knew your insensitivity would somehow get the best
of you.
What, did you think I would stand by forever and watch you
be cruel?
> You are incapable of loving anyone but yourself;
>> there is room for only one in your mirror –
> remember when the evil queen thought she was the
fairest one of all?
> You are no longer invited.

You are no longer invited.
> How dare you feign innocence.
> I can see through your sheep's clothing,
>> I am not so easily fooled.
I won't play devil's advocate any longer: you were wrong!
> Only patience is a virtue,
>> forgiveness must be earned,
> and it looks like you have tough job ahead of you now.

So I ask you:
> and you're here, why?
>> You are no longer invited.

I Don't Want To: I Can't Do It

I don't want to: I can't do it;
    you taste bitter in my mouth.
The sweet succulence of your skin dissolves on the tip of my
tongue, tasteless.
    Your impetuous kiss suffocates me.

Don't touch me: it's sadistic,
        there is no pleasure in your caress.
    It used to be gentle -
            now your tenderness only burns.

When I see you, I smile,
        you still take my breath away.
    I would love to kiss your supple lips;
    but, I'm afraid of your vicious bite -
        of swallowing one of your malignant words
                and choking on it.
                    I have suffered enough from that discourse!

I don't want to: I can't do it,
    I won't waste more time.
We need to level the playing field –
    I refuse to let you win!
You are only the booby prize,
            I am jilted with,
                    for coming in second place.

The Colors of Love

Red devours me like anger.
  Like cinnamon I fall prey to its intensity.
Harsh and dissonant
      like a child pounding on the piano –
      the sound of your voice pummels my nerves –
it's like the distant roar of thunder showers over Missouri.
Your hot and pungent breath sparks a fire in my soul.
        It burns like a raging inferno.
          It sits in my gut.
          It ravages me from the inside out.

Black consumes your heart like death.
        Death -- black as midnight on a starless eve –
          the lonely, bleak, cold air hiding love.
        Opaque emptiness alive,
                      sitting,
                          waiting - -
                                  like death.

Blue absorbs us like the deep abyss of the oceans.
    It drowns out life
                  like the way *you* drowned out life.
  Cold, abrasive hands rub down my back.
      Shivers rack my body.
        A lifeless chill haunts these waters.
Your pale, blue face is rigid.
        There is no more air.
        Water. There is nothing but water.
        Breathe it in.
              This is my love now.

I Hate You!

I hate you!
  Do you care?
  Does that mean anything?
I abhor you!
  No, I detest you.
  From you, there is always pain.
I loved you.
  Now it's useless,
  there is nothing here to gain.
I don't understand your objectives.
I can't figure out your game.
You loved me, I was certain.
Now I feel ashamed - -
and your futile tears are slighted
as you plead to me in vain.

Resentment

angry words,
malicious lies,
    spewing from your mouth,
like acid on my heart
eating away at my soul.
love is blind,
fate was tricked
   I close my eyes -
         and cry!
You run around in circles
    losing your way every time:
when will you stop and ask for directions?
this is ridiculous
   I refuse to cry -
I won't give in to your charm.
When will you understand
     it was my person
         you were in love with?
Where's the confusion in that?
     I guess someday I'll comprehend.
Until then,
   I cringe at the sound of your name:
like a secret, it is best kept silent
    whispered quietly from mouth to mouth
waiting to be revealed.

Anger Is Difficult To Eat

Anger is difficult to eat.
    With its rough edges and salty center-
        it is an unpopular delicatessen sandwich.

Anger is difficult to wear-
    like a sweater that has shrunk and no longer fits --
    I can't seem to get it over my shoulders.

Anger is difficult to hear.
    Like a stealth predator that roams at night-
    it goes undetected.
        Quietly cruising the streets,
            it looks for someone to befriend.

Anger is difficult to smell.
    It is repugnant and sour,
        like milk, which has spoiled all day in the sun-
it is unwelcome and detested,
        and in need of discard.

Anger is difficult in all of its aspects,
    it is better left alone.
  It may taunt you and ridicule you
    with promises of joy –
  but beware,
    anger is a difficult liar.

I Am Anger

I am anger!
    Use me.
    Shape me to your will.
    Bend me;
            I am your weapon!
     I am sharp.
              Prick your finger with me and watch it bleed.
                  The thin red stream - - that is me.
    I am painful.
              Watch me sting with hateful words.
                  Each one is powerful: they will never cower.
    I am vindictive.
            Belligerency causes me to smile.
              It is useless to try and persuade me.
              I won't give in.
I am anger!
    Use me.
    Make me your friend.
    Take me to meet your parents.
      Teach me how to live your life - -
           then I will destroy it.

I am anger!

I Had Every Chance To Be Strong

Why did I let you walk all over me?
I had every chance to be strong.
Did you think my heart was a welcome mat
that you could wipe your feet on?

Why did I let you control me?
I have a mind of my own!
Was it worth it, to you, for me to be
someone else you didn't know?

I had every chance to be strong,
to prove I wasn't shy.
Why did you sugarcoat your promises
if they were only sour lies?

I had every chance to be strong;
to maintain my sense of pride –
yet it wasn't I who threw in the towel
to run away and hide.

I wonder if you think about
the sacrifices I made.
Do you even think of me at all
while you go about your day?

Why did I let you walk all over me?
I had every chance to be strong.
Well, it's time to win back my dignity
to be who I was all along.

Tear

You squeeze me gently from your eye
and I give my life for you.
My only want is to see you cry
You squeeze me gently from your eye.
Your anger was your battle cry - -
your words were so untrue.
You squeeze me gently from your eye
and I give my life for you.

Section 2: Doubt

Our doubts are traitors
And make us lose the good we oft might win
By fearing to attempt

--William Shakespeare

It is almost as if I have disappeared. And the truth is I don't want to be found. I do not make any plans nor do I welcome visitors; I live in the deep, dark bowels of my home. My loved ones probably assume I'm dead – they're practically right. My soul's a barren field of dried-up anguish. *How poetic is that!*

I can't believe it's over!

I can't believe I miss you!

I took to covering up all the mirrors in the house. When I looked into them I saw only the blank reflection of rejection staring back at me: slapping me hard in the face! Maybe I should just take them all down. The mirrors used to give this place such a sparkle, especially when the sun was high in the sky and the brilliant light cascaded onto the floor and enlivened each room. Whatever! I don't want to deal with those happy reflections anymore. They're all dead as far as I'm concerned.

I have shut nearly all the windows from the world. There is nothing to see here. I don't want to be seen either. I feel tied down; tethered to the floor. My legs are heavy and I don't have the strength to move them. Besides, there is nothing out there for me, nothing but questions I am not ready to answer. I pretend to be happy, but my face shows insufferable sadness. We're over; yet, we can't be, can we? Please, someone – anyone - tell me it isn't real.

I need you. My soul feels stagnant without you. I'm like a lone buoy drowning in the middle of the ocean. Life has no purpose; I have no purpose, nothing around for miles and miles in which to validate my use in this world. So I sit here instead hoping to remain numb.

I despise the sun. I wish it wouldn't shine any more. The whole world should be desolate, dark, and lonely. As such, the murky waters of despair pulse through the streets of my life with the voraciousness of a crazed killer. It's madness! There seems to be nothing left! The world has fallen apart. The wind blows differently as if it's pushing me trying to get me out of the way. Birds hum death songs; gray clouds loom in the sky pelting pedestrians with giant rain-tears. It feels as if the sun fell to earth and started a fire - - I'll just sit here and pray it consumes me soon.

Ironically, I am so tired of being in this room, but I can't seem to leave it. Everything about it is lifeless and, like me, seems to have no will to exist. Even the paint is struggling to cling to the walls when it looks like it would rather flake and crumble to the floor at any moment. Some days I feel like that as well. I sit here day after day waiting for you to return. I know how foolish I would look to someone just sitting here and how insensitive you are for giving me this reason to be so forlorn. You've been gone for so long: so, so long. The hours go slowly. The ticking of the second hand on the clock punishes me like Chinese water torture, each tick drawing angry curses to submit to a solitary life without you.

Sitting here I remember the happiness this room once embraced: the sofa so eager to comfort you, to ease the stress of your day; pictures of our life together – several vacation trips and a couple of holidays, like those with your family – I haven't quite had the heart to take down yet; and various tchotchke items representing your presence – they are all here day after day as well. But what about me? What is there to kill my anguish as these things stare back at me? I can hear their shrill laughter even now as if they knew your intentions all along. How could they figure anything out before I did?

My whimpers are thunder in the house. I take a deep breath and hold it for several seconds. I should just forget to breathe overall but instead release it. Then I take another breath to block my tears. The somber violin with its desolate melody echoes the sentiments of my heart. How deplorable its voice is when spoken in a hushed whisper. Oh how magnificent the violin accompanies the melancholy woes of life. In this composition, *I* am the violin playing the underscore to *your* exit.

I can't believe it's over.

I can't believe I miss you!

I can't believe my sorrow cracks through this empty hell and shatters the threads of my dignity.

I can't believe I let you, let me feel this way.

And I can't believe it's time to move on.

More To Say

Life is left in deep dismay
I am your sordid past
There is nothing more to say

You just up and went away
So many questions never asked
Life is left in deep dismay

I am stranded, in love, like a castaway
In misery's company does every hour pass
There is nothing more to say

The hue of day is shadowed in gray
The clouds are shrewd, alas!
Life is left in deep dismay

To believe your heart could ever sway
That your apathy might surpass
There is nothing more to say

Somewhere, once, you were led astray
As I am your sordid past
Life is left in deep dismay
There is nothing more to say

I Feel Like I'm Losing

I know it's not a competition;
yet, I feel like I'm losing.

I know it isn't a game,
    that you need some time away;
  but I still feel like I'm losing.

Each day you get farther away.
    Seeing me,
        being near me,
            reminds you of why your soul is in pain.
        That is not my fault;
            yet, I sense that somehow I'm to blame.
You turn off your emotions –
        (like ignoring love has ever solved anything in the
past.)
    Well I feel like I'm losing.
                    I don't know what to do!

I wish I could hug you;
    secure you in my arms,
        until the tempest passes,
        that rages out of control
        inside your mind.

I wish my love were a weapon
    which you could use in your fight;
my faith and support the armor
    that protected you through the night.

Instead I feel I'm losing -
    my armory going untouched;
you abandon all hope of faith
    and pray to survive from luck.

I know it's not a competition,
   or a battle for your love,
   that you're as scared as I am;
but I feel like I'm losing
      because I'm here for you –
         next to you;
      yet, you look the other way.

I Don't Want To Cry

Please don't think I don't love you.
  My breath waits in anticipation
        to see your smiling face.
  My heart beats with a quenchless desire
      at the mention of your name,
    like the thirsty cactus in the desert sun
        extinguished by indiscernible rage.
I would hold you close if the warmth of my body
    helped you sleep at night.
    The truth is,
        I love you very much.
    The fact is,
        I don't want to cry anymore.
        I don't want to sleep in an empty bed or in
        a cold embrace;
            why even turn my way if all you're
going to do is look right through me?
        If my hugs have the meaning of just a pat on the back,
        then why have outstretched arms?
I don't want to cry anymore,
        I have no more tears to shed.
  My eyes only squelch out dust,
  which blows back in my face,
        burns my eyes,
  and reminds me of our past.
I don't want to cry anymore.
We sit in silence, *together*, in the same room.
        I can't believe there is nothing left to say!
Actually, I have plenty to say;
            you refuse to listen.
My words once had meaning,
        your actions took heed…
and now we both refuse to care.
    My utterances are nothing more than rambled
questions
      spouted to plead acceptance.
        Your actions are cold and pragmatic.
        You stand with tenacious egotism,
    as if your answers are the *answers* above all answers.

I don't want to cry,
 I won't ask why -
I don't want to know anymore.
      I love you like the stars love the night sky - -
                              it's providential;
      yet, somehow that doesn't seem to be enough.
I can't take it.
      If we can't talk to each other,
         than what use is it to try,
  because I can love you in silence -
              but I refuse to go it alone.

Remember Me?

Remember me?
I listen - I care.
I win in the end.
    Does that make me smug?
I'm the one with the broken heart.
You're the one with nothing to lose
            so eager to walk away.
Do you feel brave with your back turned to me?

Remember me?
I love – I hurt.
My heart bleeds through open wounds.
    Does that make me human?
You're the one ignoring me.
I'm the one on my knees: insistent, earnest.
     Should I feel ashamed?
I don't need you, I want you.
You don't want me…you don't need me…

Need

It's more than a need.
It's more than settling for death.
It's a yearning drive that compels me to roll out of bed
day after day with a broken heart.
It's the desire to be tortured ruthlessly so it can ease against
the agony
of this burning in my beating chest:
to turn and know that you're not there;
to blink my eyes again and again and again
because I can't seem to convince myself
that you're gone.
It's more than a need.
It's more than the anticipation of lightning in a rainstorm.
It's the hunger for love,
the craving for attention.
It is the longing to look into your eyes again;
it is the undying wish to hear your voice;
it's the hopeful chance that the next time I blink
you'll be standing there
and that I was either imagining everything
or that it was just all a dream.

I Hear Shakespeare

I hear Shakespeare echo in my mind:

Cowards die many times before their deaths;
The Valiant never taste of death but once –

        and yet I am frozen,
           and I am unable to move.
        I am a coward.

I have tasted death on countless occasions
      for we have danced often
and sat on cool winter nights discussing
          politics, religion, and the secrets of life - -
and He has patiently waited by my side during long
      summer days while I contemplated His philosophies.
I have felt the breath of courage on my face as she walked
with me in the dark – out in front – tempting me to grab for
her and always just out of reach!

I am Shakespeare's words
    in flesh and in bone,
      shrouded in silence
hidden among timorous lies
   as the truth marched ahead without me,
      unaware of my confusion,
as I was dragged along behind in its glory.

I hear Shakespeare echo in my mind.
I question his integrity to understand my perception
  that I am a coward who dares to dream of chivalrous honor
      without savoring the agony of defeat
         or the success of failure,
for I am a coward.

I hear Shakespeare echo in my mind.......

Atheist

Is there a God?
   Who answers my call when I pray?
   Who witnesses my good deeds?
   Who forgives my sins?

Is there no God?
   When I cry, alone at night, who will wipe my tears away?
   Who can I tell my dreams to?
   Who will know my pain?

No - - there is no God!
   There is no Heaven
         and there is no Hell.
   Dreams are only answered from a shooting star,
         and if you wish hard and long enough
         and believe with your whole soul
               then fate will show you the way.

Is there no God?
      As the plague of doubted ignorance erases innocence
         who will call to the people to arise against oblivion?
      When faith is cloaked in simple lies
            and misguided tongues lead the way,
   then who will help the weary wanderers find the right path?

I look to the sky.
         Tears fill my eyes.
            I don't know why
                  I need to cry -
         but I do.
If there is no God to believe in me,
then why should I believe in Him?

Amazing

Amazing how life changes in a moment
  In the blink of an eye
                so much time has passed -
                so much wasted on frivolity;
        strangers who have passed
                and ne'er a single word uttered in their direction.
  Fathers, brothers, mothers,
                a neighbor's dying aunt whose day
                you never took the opportunity to shine.
Amazing how life changes in a moment.
        You close your eyes,
                    weary from the toil of the sun,
and you've missed a week, a month,
            the laugh of a child,
                  the *one* person who cared enough
                    to stand there in front of you
                        arms stretched open
                    waiting to be embraced,
            and the plague of silence
                        and despair
            pulled you farther and farther away.
Amazing how life changes in a moment.
    Each morning is welcomed with a brand new sun -
            new stories,
            new anecdotes of youthful charm,
        old friends with new memories -
    and years have passed
    and still the same dreams haunt you.
Amazing how life changes in a moment.
        And it's over.....
                    just as quickly as it began!

The Path To Hell

The path to hell is paved with good intentions
    and good intentions are noble tasks.
Nobility is practiced acceptance
        disguised as content.
  I have opened Pandora's box and,
           with sword in hand,
        am waiting for the next demon to strike.
The darkness is sweltering with the dreams no one has ever dreamt,
      and like captured prey,
        I fight against their torment.
I am powerless against the magic of their charm
      and am left to adopt each one:
      motherless children screaming into the abyss of their
imagination,
their hollow echoes dying in the staleness of their minds;
       abandoned memories left on the side of the road
          to rot and die in the heat;
        lost, sacred souls of the unbelievers who haunt the
          halls of the Earth - -
    each one plays on my soul
            bringing me down kicking and yelling.
I wish I knew how to break free.
       They all grab at me and pull me under.
    I am drowning!
And the path to Hell is paved with good intentions
     and good intentions are noble tasks.
  But it's probably good to forget the past...
        yet it's always biting,
           biting, biting at my heels.
The path to Hell is cold and lonely;
       I'm better off turning back and heading home.

Towards The Finish Line

I can see the finish line.
  I run and run as it gets farther away.
I take a deep breath
          and begin to sprint.
      My legs burn,
              but I want it so badly I can taste it.
        The smell of victory comes to me in the breeze.
        It entices me.
          I push harder. I hurl my body forward.
I can see the finish line.
        My body aches.
        My pores sweat.
        My legs scream;
            I will not stop.
            I can't stop.
     The other runners have finished.
    They are cheering me on. They give me confidence.
Slowly the sun sets in the soft pink sky.
      I will continue running –
          I have come too far; I am way too close.
I can see the finish line. I can see the finish line!
    I push harder. I want to make it.
  Then I stumble.
        The ground, underneath, gives way.
           I fall. I trip. I land.
The dirt is dry in my mouth.
My chest heaves with each breath.
  I know I should give up.
  I want to give up!
        I can see the finish line.
     It is deserted. The audience has gone,
    and the silence they left behind is deafening.
     But I will not let them win.

The sun breaks through the dull night sky
and I get up and run.
My body aches.
My pores sweat.
My legs scream,
but I will not stop.
I will not stop.
I run towards the finish line
and this time I will succeed,
but the more I run the farther it becomes.

Section 3: Isolation / Depression

When you come to the edge of all the light you have known, and you are about to step out into darkness, Faith is knowing one of two things will happen – there will be something to stand on, or you will be taught to fly.

--Jonathan Livingston Seagull

Cold, dark corridors – long – with no end in sight, continuing on and on into oblivion. Chilly waters trickle down the wall; moss seeps out from within the rock barricades on either side of me; mildew reaches out to me like a poor, wretched vagrant hungry for food: repugnant as rotting meat. The stench is thick and heavy as it follows me. I shiver. Fires of passions burning in my core – ignited deep within my soul have since died; leaving only smoldering ashes and a wintry chill of loneliness. The bleak hollow passageways lie ahead of me like a constant reminder of my past failures. All I seek is comfort from their familiar, safe paths. They listen silently to my heart's weeping. I am alone!

What is isolation?

The dull throbbing pain in my heart; the vast and infinite sigh accompanying each breath; the absence of life. It is a loveless void. Isolation is the final exhale; the bellow of my voice echoing off these walls and fading, unnoticed, into the background.

I walk into the streets of my neighborhood like a stealth intruder. No one acknowledges my presence. So many people surround me; yet I feel so alone. So truly and utterly alone – *I* am isolation!

Can this all be a dream? Mere curiosity forces me to aimlessly wander these channels. It silently takes my hand and leads me through these dark tunnels. My feet just follow. We move together towards the deepening fog. At first a light mist closes out the world beyond my peripheral vision, but it gradually becomes denser. It's nearly impenetrable. I have nowhere else to go so I keep walking. I choke on my heart as it jumps into my throat and tries to flee. Ha! How ignorant my heart is! So many mistakes it has made before, and yet it refuses to listen to experience. Insanity governs this ferocious beast. It fights to escape the chalky nothingness, which keeps us imprisoned, refusing quiet surrender.

I want to run but I don't know which path would lead me out of this dark, dank hole. Everything is gray. In fact, the more I breathe in the vapor the grayer *I*, myself, become. I am beginning to blend in with the surrounding, quickly becoming a faceless entity. I am now no different than other shapeless, nameless masses surrounding me. We are many and yet we are alone. *We* are all isolated.

Isolation!

I don't know where this path is going. I can't even be sure when it will end, for it seems to continue and continue forever. I am trapped! I wish I could leave or just step to the side and somehow miraculously fall off this well beaten trail. I have walked it for many years – so many moons have come and gone since I began this journey. I am still here! There is no destination; I am a traveler who has neither departed nor arrived. I am lost without a hope of ever being found. I will disappear into the fog only to be forgotten by all who know me.

Isolation – Solitude – Detachment – the loneliness of an echo with no one to hear – the abandoned hopelessness of a single tear vociferated in despair – the hollow emptiness of a thousand passages, which never seems to end. Boundless, vacant chambers depleted of affectivity, only to be left with a dull, aching disinterest that wounds the heart and leaves it to bleed interminably....

Reasonable Doubt

I am a criminal without a crime
running with guilt on my shoulders
a burden slowing me down
leaving fingerprints on everything I touch
my words hidden clues left to solve a mystery - -
like a story told out of order
thrown into the climax with no release,
beginning with a dénouement
that fails to answer any questions,
ending with a prologue,
which introduces bland, over-used characters - -
so there is nothing left but a misshaped jigsaw puzzle.
I am the last piece missing when it is almost completed
obliterated somewhere in oblivion
knowing that I am needed to finish the picture
snickering because I am running and running
and running
with guilt on my shoulders
stuck in the quicksand
swallowed in half by the mouth of nature
clawing and clawing to reach for a dangling vine,
which rears its head –
all scales
venomous teeth
a forked tongue aimed for my eyes
a piece of cottontail wedged in the back of its throat
coming towards me like Lucifer –
evil in its eyes –
prepared to fight another Great Battle
this time with nothing to lose
wearing vengeance like a necktie
a noose that is wound tight with precision,
which I use to hang myself with in mid-air
and suspend my feet over a dying cause.
I am a just barbarian
a bigot with no one to judge
a riot of people who write notes back and forth to each other
because their voices have no power.

This is the end of the line
and to jump would mean to
fall prey to incendiary hands
that are as soft and as gentle as lamb's wool
but as subtle as a plane crash
as genuine as the first spark of a raging fire.
Taking a deep breath
I inhale the fumes of gasoline
and I dive head first into the flames.
I am a criminal without a crime
running with guilt on my shoulders
and the burden is far greater,
is far more overwhelming
than the proof of reasonable doubt.

The Edge Of The World

I am standing on the edge of the world
    and the little sliver of moon
    reaches across the water
like a faint shadow
        in the deep, black forever-ness all around me.
There is a lone buoy ringing out there – somewhere –
    perhaps its hollow drum-drum
        an echo of my empty heart.
I am standing on the edge of the world
    and the night breeze bites at my cheeks.
      They are red and chapped from its coarse lips.
      My nose is numb and tender when I touch it
and I am drawn to the vast openness before me:
        the stars that twinkle and call for me.
      They watch me with stellar patience,
  as if my eyes weren't the only eyes that they have ever
looked into.
I am standing on the edge of the world
    looking out into the dark
      as if there were a hidden treasure
    and that if I were to close my eyes and walk blindly
      I could *and* would stumble upon it.
I am standing on the edge of the world;
    all there is, is an infinite amount of sand
  with footprints that lead to eternity
and the celestial silence of a million years,
    which fades away behind me
    as I turn around
      and walk away.

Searching

The black clouds above presage a thunderstorm.
   The quick and constant flash of lightning forebodes my doom.
The sky-high walls of green shrubbery
  protect the outside world - -
      as they suffocate me within.
Rabid raindrops fall like bullets aimed at the target on my back.
         These passages seem to last forever.
         The darkness is endless as I hustle along.
I hear faint sounds in the distance:
      Is it a muffled cry?
         A smothered scream?
            Perhaps it's a subdued, muted rustling in the thicket?
I run! That's all I have left;
               my last device for survival.
The rain comes down faster and faster.
   It sticks to me like wax.
    It weighs down my arms and my legs.
I close my eyes for there is nothing to see - -
  each corner leads me nowhere,
      every corridor looks the same.
Fear overwhelms me.
      It frequents regularly -
         I often fancy it part of my attire,
            much like that of a coat or a pair of shoes.
I stumble; I struggle to get up.
   I catch my breath.
The sound of my respiring echoes
  and its resonance is foreign to my ears.
I look around.
      I've been here before! All of this seems familiar.
Why do I always run when I know the hallway never ends?
When is the confusion replaced with acceptance?
   What the hell am I searching for anyway?
         I pause. I take another deep breath and turn around: this time, my journey,
                  will start in the other direction.

The Seduction Of Fear

Suffer the innocence standing on the threshold of life
    and held by the desire of fear.
      The sweet succulence of the known, comfortable path
       worn down by the daily toil of monogamous footsteps.
      To stand on that plateau and see the bird free to fly
       the Heavens,
   and to look down at my healthy vibrant wings, which
cease to have the soothing winds ruffle its feathers.
Suffer the insolence of a fool eager to taste the wine
       without ever squashing a single grape,
   leaving them to grow and then die on the same vine,
       the desire of fear pulsating like the ripples in
        stagnant water.
Suffer the frustrated protagonist
     too ashamed to write his story,
      to act out each word,
        to comprehend each scripted moment,
    who would rather flip the pages of the book
     to see what the reader sees.
Suffer the damned soul that is carted to ethereal eternity
      forced to watch each sordid memory
       played over again and again to
        a lifeless audience.
      Silence the award of bittersweet agony
       set out like a bowl of fruit for
        everyone to pick at,
          to tear away
         and discard as human waste.
Suffer the innocence standing on the threshold of life
    and held by the desire of fear,
  unable to free from its grasp,
    looking ahead at the path of the future,
   turning to the past for some sort of recognition
and knowing that failure is as simple
      as sitting down in the middle
     and letting the heart descend to oblivion
    without a parachute.

Missing You

I.

The room is silent without you.
Where are you?
I have looked all over - -
        I can't find you;
        I want to cry.
The cup of tea that you didn't drink
    waits for you on the table.
It's getting cold,
        and I'm missing you.
You were my favorite dolly.
          I can't fall asleep without you.

II.

The sound of my breathing echoes in the darkness.
I can't see anything.
I'm too afraid to move
      so I just lie here listening.
        It's quiet.
       I'm scared
         and I'm missing you.
When you are here; you take the shadows away.
When you are here
        I know the boogey man can't get me:
   I think he's allergic to light.

III.

I don't know what to do.
Where are you?
I see other people walk by –
        they are taller than me –
    they don't look like you!
Where are you? Why did you leave?
There are tall walls – in front and behind –
        I can't see around them
          and I'm missing you.
"Mommy!" I shout. "Mommy, where are you?"
    I'm crying really loud so you'll hear me.
        Please come find me.
            I think I'm in the cereal aisle.
              Hurry!

IV.

I don't care.
    I don't want you to go.
I'll cling to your leg.
I won't let go.
I'm crying to show you I'm serious (and scared).
    What is school anyway?
    I have blocks like this at home.
    Why can't we go home?
  You're not even gone yet
      and I'm missing you.
    I don't want to play with the other kids.
    I have friends at home.
    Why can't we go home?

V.

I don't understand!
How can you be my daddy
        if you don't love mommy?
                Mommy cries so much.
                Why does mommy cry?
                She doesn't know I can hear her
                        but I can.
                So many tears, daddy,
                she cries at night.
                Always at night!
        She sounds like a ghost moaning so loud
                and I'm missing you.
I don't understand.
        Why does mommy cry
                when I'm still here?

Sixteen-Year-Old Face

I can no longer remember the time
when I could look in the mirror
     and see my sixteen-year-old face staring back at me.
  The twinkle has lost its luster.
  The windows to the soul are hard to see through
    from worn out yellowed glass.
My face is so dry and cracked now.
Sometimes I stare at myself in disbelief:
  this person staring back is *not* me.
There is still a faint trace of that youthful vigor when I smile,
but most of it is buried at the bottom
      of a thousand memories.
How heavy they make my eyes look.
How they have stretched my skin from the daily lifting
  and tugging of the history of my life.
I can recall each one though as if they all happened
the previous day:
      The house was full of laughter then.
      The row of sunflowers that lined the streets
        signaling the beginning of spring.
     And back then, when I looked in the mirror,
 I could remember the face of the sixteen-year-old
     reflecting back at me.
       It was a bit older, a little wiser
       but under the strain of adulthood
       you could make out the adolescent charm.
Now I can no longer remember the time
  when I could look in the mirror
    and see my sixteen-year-old face staring back at me.
   It has faded along with the laughter,
    retreated into the pile of memories
    that I carry everyday.
And yet these memories can't make my house warm.
  They haunt my dreams with vivid pictures,
   begging me to reach out for them:
     to visit old friends
     my first kiss
the summer nights in the tall grass looking up at the stars—
each one flickers past

faster and faster and faster and faster.
I can no longer remember the time
    when I could look in the mirror
and see my sixteen-year-old face staring back at me.
     Did it ever exist?
And if I were to search through all the reminiscences
I've collected –
     would I even recognize it anymore after all this time?

In My Dreams

In my dreams I am a fugitive slave
    suppressed from freedom
  by the constant fear of capture.
The pitch black of night is my truest friend
    and my darkest foe.
  Each sound startles me
     and sets alive each nuance of my nerve endings.
   I only breathe when I have to.
   I stop running only when I need to.

In my dreams I am an eagle soaring high above the
mountains.
    The blue sky stretches out before me
     in an endless cerulean sea.
   I could fly for days and see the same waves
     crashing against the clouds,
      and rushing back out into the vast azure plain.
    The wind rushes past as if racing.
    My screech never replies in echo
     for there is nothing to receive its call.

In my dreams I am a scarecrow
  with a straw hat that shields against the squelching sun.
   Big, fat, lazy, crows perch on my arms
    and nibble on my straw,
  while they *caw-caw* gossip in the noonday heat.
They don't speak to me.
   I don't understand their words.
   They just come and go like familiar,
                unwelcome friends.

Swimming The Storm

At first our love was like the shallow end
   in the cascade blue still-waters of a swimming pool.
The surface was undisturbed and totally inviting
            as is the beginning of love.
I swam in your waters,
        and floated with your waves
               as I dove into your arms!
At first,
      our love was like the gentle gliding of a canoe
           across the silken green lake,
        the synchronized rowing of the oars
            that lifted the vessel across the ripples.
Our love was the free-flowing
          deluge of a waterfall
      crashing over the rocky edge
      and feeding into the lagoon.
Love was the swan - -
         elegant, beautiful, and graceful:
       something precious to behold;
           yet dainty and too delicate to touch.
Now, love is the deep end
      and the torrent, churning tides try to pull me under.
I stroke,
     I kick, I paddle
      and I can barely keep my head above the surface.
         I gasp for air.
       Loving you was like drowning –
the passion as rough as a hurricane
        wiping out small villages
        leaving casualties wherever we went - -
everyone was affected by our love:
         the way you stroked my hair
         the way I embraced your lips with mine,
how you would drag me along like a little steam boat into the
harbor
and leave me adrift, sometimes, in the open sea.

Now,
  our love is the remains after an apocalyptic tidal wave.
    Nothing is recognizable.
    Nothing remains the same,
        and we are left to rebuild an empire
        from just a few scraps of wood.

One Love

I whisper in the dark,
   while lying in bed
      just to hear a voice.
I wrap my arms around myself
         so I can have skin against my skin.
I light candles
   so there are other shadows cast on the wall
 and I play jazz with a sultry bass line
   to coincide with the slow
     rhythm of my heart.
I feed myself grapes
       and berries
    and I moan loudly every time I take one in my mouth
    because they are *so* good!
I sleep with huge pillows all around me
   and in the middle of the night
   I roll over and hug them for warmth.
I listen to love songs
     and slow dance around the living room
   with my arms high above my head
 swaying like large palm trees in the warm, tropical breeze.
  And I can imagine myself sitting on the beach
   on some distant island,
      out where no one can find me,
    while the sun caresses my bare body.
I pick beautiful roses
    and place them in a vase
      on the center of my dining-room table
    and delight in the fragrance they give so freely
    to the stale, quietness of my home.
I smile when I'm sad
   to confuse my heart
    and trick it into thinking differently - -
      and so far it hasn't caught on!

I write myself poems and hang them on my walls.
They have eloquent versus like…
"…the sand of time phases into the
light of your eyes,
and the touch of your hand
on the back of my neck
reminds me of young children laughing,
and couples kissing,
or the sweet scent of jasmine
in the springtime –
and when I close my eyes,
even when you're not there,
I can see your face,
for I have memorized its beauty
and carry it with me like a portrait in my mind…"
I draw hot baths with petals of purple orchids
and let my mind wander with their aroma
as it sends me to far off places I've never been
and always yearn to return to.
I drink hot chocolate,
with a stick of cinnamon,
by the fireplace.
I read books out loud:
stories of lost travelers who explore the world,
wandering down muddy rivers,
or through dense forests,
and sleep under the glittery sky,
or in the rain - -
wrapping their arms around themselves
so that they have skin against their skin,
and forget,
like me,
that they are alone.

Dreaming

The world is mythological.
The colors of reality blend together
with the words of imagination
uniting in compassion;
like the sun and moon,
who converse with obeisant assurance,
they speak of tranquil afternoons --
as we sit together
on the back of a butterfly
and rise over a cascading waterfall.
Silence laments to the solitude.
Obscurity suffocates life.
With the frailty of a feather,
we fall, fall, fall into the black abyss
swallowed by the emptiness of a world,
which ceases to exist.
Landing on the cotton softness of a cloud,
we exult in the brilliance of the Heavens!
Around us is the warmth of light,
the breath of grandeur,
the testimony of everlasting fellowship.
Here we are the living testament,
we see the scripture of unheard memories.
We take with us the keys to open all locked doors.
We will keep the answers in our hearts,
where they will forever be safe.
We no longer have to rely on deceptive allegory,
and we will now be empowered to turn into ourselves for
redemption.
We close our eyes.

We open our eyes.

There before us are the trees. *They know the secret.*
There before us is the dandelion. *It knows the secret.*
 The otter. The monkey. The squirrel. *They all know.*
The world is united in compassion.
 Knowledge is power.
 Fear is oppression. It blinds the truth.
The sun,
 once again,
 takes reign over the sky
 and life awakens with a new grasp of existence.

Good-Bye

Why must there be disease?
    The reality of death is so close at hand - -
        why must I watch Him from the window
   dancing there in the soft light of a half visible moon
        soaking in the black waters of the night?
He is so beautiful.
              I have seen his face before. In my dreams.
              I have wished on every cloud that has
                  acquiesced to the sun's delight
                  just to look into those eyes again.

Why must there be pain?
    The fire flows from within and burns my skin
         scalding, hot, oozy lava
             wounded
             broken
      doubled-over, intense, so bad I can barely stand
Why must there be pain?

Why must I say good-bye?
   Good-bye is so final,
              so complete,
         so informal,
            so unforgiving
      never having a second chance to say hello again.

Why is it so black?
Why am I so cold –
        then warm –
      then happy –
    then no longer afraid of disease
       no longer afraid of pain
       no longer afraid of saying good-bye?

Section 4: Acceptance / Faith

I slip back many times,
I fall, I stand still, I run against the edge of
hidden obstacles,
I lose my temper and find it again and
keep it better.
I trudge on, I gain a little, I feel
encouraged,
I get more eager and climb higher and
begin to see the widening horizon.
Every struggle is a victory.

--Helen Keller

While cleaning the hidden debris and dust lingering behind the couch, I found a picture of you. Until then, I hadn't realized that I had nearly forgotten what you had looked like – almost. Oddly enough, I still think you're attractive: the lines around your eyes while you laughed, the little dimple haughtily embossed on your cheek, pouty lips begging to be kissed. Wow, how I had longed for them when I had first met you. Yet, looking at this fossilized replication of your face doesn't affect my balance as it once did when I would look at it. I gently blow the dust from your portrait, watching it scatter like a storm cloud, finally exposing a long forgotten secret.

I don't know how your picture got behind the couch - but there you were lying like a misplaced trinket or a piece of gaudy jewelry abandoned for its lack of accessory.

Finally, I throw open the drapes letting the warm sun squeeze through the window and stretch its legs out across the floor. It lifts its arms to the ceiling quickly replacing the stale, dead air that I had inhaled for so long. Now, the furniture and the walls feel alive again, useful in splendor glory rather than desolate sorrow. I became desperate to wipe away the grime of depression and fatigue, sweep up the dried up tears that collected on the floor, and diminish the fragrance of failure and feigned ignorance. This is the passing of mourning.

A faint smile crosses my lips while looking at your picture. You look familiar, almost like kin; yet your face is so startling and unreal. I know we used to know each other, but it seems as if it almost didn't happen - - almost. And looking around the house, there is nothing noticeable of your presence any longer save this picture. Funny, isn't it? How I had cried so many tears, sat in utter silence in this very room, and prayed that the only visitor would be Death himself finally delivering me from this Hell and taking me to another lonelier, unimaginable Hell – if indeed, such a place could have been worse than this. And yet, after all that, I almost didn't remember your face - - almost.

There were times when I'd walk around a corner sharply and thought I saw you out of the corner of my eye. That was your memory, which realized that it was no longer accepted here and left. Your voice echoed once as well, but it was only the wind howling through the cracks. I'm used to the sound now.

I tried baking an apple pie once too. Even put cinnamon in it to capture that perfect taste. Ah cinnamon. It was difficult at first – almost. I didn't even think I could take a bite of it for fear that my effort would be in vain. It was magnificent though. I had forgotten that apple pie was my favorite. I eat it a little bit differently now, with a scoop of ice cream on top. It's ironic how some things never leave us.

Nope, this picture is all that's left. I can't even place where you were when it was taken. Was I there or was this one brought when you moved in? Oh well, it doesn't matter now. That is in the past. The past is over and with it the shreds of torn, faded memories. And I tear your picture into fragments such as those past projections and let them fly out the window in the warm afternoon breeze. The last thing I see is one scrap of your eye as it sits on the grass twitching under the searing sun before it's lifted and carried away. It was like you wanted one last look, something to take with you, before it was all over. I laugh at this, a little guttural snort, at the irony of the situation. You never looked back when you left. This was your moment of truth. I *will* be okay! Even though my heart isn't back to normal, it still beats with a steady triumphant rhythm. I know that someday soon – very soon – it will heal completely and the only thing of you that will forever remain is a little scar no one will ever see.

Someone

Someone love me!
      Someone place caressing hands on my cheeks
            to remind me I'm alive.
      Someone look into my eyes and explore my world,
          which lies beyond their thick hazel barricade.
      Someone yearn for my lips,
              hunger and crave my kiss,
  pray for the slight whisper of my voice across your neck.

Someone love me!
      Someone tear down my walls
and lead me through this valley of fear.
         I cannot walk it alone.
      Someone touch me – hot flesh against hot flesh –
                  soul against soul.
        Hold me close. Teach me to embrace myself.
          Someone kiss the small of my back,
            taste each curve of my thigh,
          savor the crevice in the bend of my arm.

Someone love me!
         Notice the warmth of my smile,
             how it draws you in,
          pulls you closer, closer, closer.
      Someone understand my pain
          and then learn to navigate its course.
  Learn my language. Share my blessings.
Someone close their eyes and anticipate my laughter.

Someone love me!
      Someone cherish me.
        I am a frightened child - -
          swaddle me in your acceptance
           and devotion towards life.

Someone love me!
      Someone... someone...
         some...
           one...
            ...me...

Speaking To Me

My heart is speaking to me,
    and for so long I haven't listened to what it was saying.
It would beat madly like a raving lunatic
      and I would try to calm it with poetry,
          and literature, and soft ballads I would
            sing in my head.
    I would soothe it by weeping
        and flood my hands with the sweet nectarine
          that flowed from within;
    and yet, it would never stop its frightening pulse.
Sometimes it would barely beat at all,
          never aspiring to do its heart duty
        too exhausted to even move.
My heart is speaking to me
    and for so long I haven't listened to what it was saying.
It has wanted to tell me stories
          but I wouldn't stay to hear the end.
    It has wanted to hold a conversation
        and I wouldn't engage in its banter.
        I wouldn't speak its name.
      I would just run and run and ignore it
        until I fell down beside it exhausted
          and too tired to hear its words.
My heart is speaking to me
    and for so long I haven't listened to what it was saying.
    I do not know if we speak the same language
      but then –
         I have never wanted to find out.
I never ask how it is doing,
        I have never tried to be its friend - -
    but my heart continued speaking to me
and for so long I haven't listened to what it was saying.

Winter Wind

The summer's blaze has been extinguished.
Brown autumn leaves flit from their safe haven
and take refuge on the grass –
languid and brittle
from the scorching heat -
mourning the existence of another time
put to rest.
The cold creeps in,
soft and subtle, at first, like a panther on the prowl
patiently waiting for the unprepared.
The rich blue of the sky is transformed to an opaque gray,
and the effervescence of life
is receded into hibernation.
Sweaters and overcoats;
mittens and scarves:
this is the garb of protection from the chill.
Introduced to the season of giving,
the time of thankfulness - -
there is a chance to reflect on blithe ponderences
of the labor we have invested in life.
Just as nature sleeps to restore its spirit,
our élan is swept away by the winter wind,
leaving a clean slate - -
a fresh canvas - -
in which to paint new pictures.

Nature's Bounty

Roses are red,
violets are blue,
pansies are purple
in the morning dew.

The new maiden sun
that broke through the night,
rises quickly above
with all its might.

The cool, crispy air
the soft, gentle breeze,
are elegantly woven
with delicate ease.

The crickets subside
with their splendorous song,
so the birds of the morning
can sing to the dawn.

A furry little rabbit,
a bushy-tailed squirrel
are aroused from their slumber
to embrace the world.

The trees stretch their limbs,
and the clouds wide awake
admire their fashion
in their reflection off the lake.

Nature's bounty is fruitful
at the touch of day's light - -
the simple breath of sunrise
is the commencement of life.

I Belong Here

I.

When the soft shadow
of silky desire
    quietly slips between
     raucous achievers
     and waxen observers,
fevered grooms find invisible brides.

II.

There is beauty through desperation
and disregarded desire
the reflection –
      in part –
     patiently waits with delicious passing
under watching trees.

III.

From such desire
    love does reach another shadow
a place never remembered,
      which the confused cannot interlude.
          I belong here!

I Am The Moon

spherical angel against the black cavern
          hungry for life
I am tormented constantly with the
          subtle layers of your passion
                    that,
                              from me,
                    you strip away
               leaving me bare and breathless
                    your thirst for carnal love
                              bestial
your kiss so tender and delicate that it makes me cry
          lips so soft and sweet,
                    like licking cotton candy
          your flesh hot, wet,
                              raging like desert heat,
                    burning against my flesh,
                              branding me with your kisses,
                              which sear deep into my side
your salty sweat stinging my tongue
                    reminding me of the warm afternoon
               looking out into the edge of the World
          and life rushing back towards me,
                    quick,
                         crashing,
                              eager to grab at my toes,
                                   my legs,
                                        my thighs,
                    yearning to taste my calves - -
the moon so high
          searching for the Goddess
          puppeteering the game
          invoking emotion
                    writing the roles of our bodies

your mouth caressing my neck
      familiarizing my earlobes with your
           sensitive touch
       exploring the curves, hills, and valleys
        of the uncharted Nile.
I am the full moon.
      I am the body.
         I am the Goddess. Worship me!

A Kiss

A kiss – a simple gesture
can say so many things:
it is the single light of darkness,
it is truth, which never fades.

It is the tender touch of petals
that are silk against the skin,
it is every wish that's ever made;
   repentance of every sin.

It is but one last breath so deeply breathed
when air is desire;
for is there anything as powerful
to squelch the raging fire?

Life -- A Circle

Life is like a circle.
It is continuous and never-ending;
constantly ending at the beginning
and beginning at the end –
it flows naturally like the spring
water, which runs down the mountain.
On its journey it picks up remnants
of life – simple inhabitants hitching a ride –
particles of sand that it deposits
farther along,
helping to build the earth
to reinforce its base.

Life is like a circle.
It is continuous and never-ending,
the beginning, the middle, and the end.
We flow naturally like a spring –
we pass along remnants of our life.
Through others: we are alive in their
memories and in the stories they tell,
and through our children that cherish our laughter,
these are the particles of our soul that we deposit
farther along the road,
helping to build the earth
to reinforce its base.

There is a rainbow - as immense as the blue sky itself-, which stretches from one end of the cerulean atmosphere to the other. It's magnificent. After the torrential rains, it's astonishing to see something so simple as a rainbow. It gives a sense of comfort, a spark of warmth. It extends into the sky reaching beyond into infinity. It doesn't look back but continues onward and onward with the confidence that wherever it's going, it needs to be there.

It's providential; it's always there. So many forget, give up hope, throw in the towel, find it so hard to continue – but after swimming the storm, I look up and there it is: a brilliant smile from Heaven, always recognizable, always welcomed. It's amazing how it breaks through the turbulence – the angry, wretched, grey clouds thrashing on one side and the beautiful, calm, freshly absolved blueness on the other – and in between a great barrier of strength that embraces both halves, as it is a combination of both pieces.

I willingly embrace this rainbow. We are friends. We have lunch and talk about the past – we laugh. It's all so funny now. I never thought I would be so happy to have the sun touch my skin and kiss at the nape of my neck. I never imagined the blue sky would radiate with the warmth of a brand new day – but we laugh. The rainbow and I are friends. Alas! That beautiful rainbow is my long, lost friend.

I wanted the perfect ending.
Now I've learned, the hard way,
that some poems don't rhyme, and some stories
don't have a clear beginning, middle, and end.

– – Gilda Radner

ACKNOWLEDGEMENTS

When I sat down one day to thank all of those who had helped me with this book, I was alarmed with the amount of people that I was truly blessed to know and with whom had touched my life. The next task was to figure out a way to extend my gratitude to these wonderful individuals who carried me through this six year journey. And what a journey it was. Six turbulent, long years with many little guardian angels who soothed and comforted me as I trekked and trudged begrudgingly along this path. But alas! I've arrived.

Who's ready for the next step?

First, I would love to thank my parents, Donald and Reta Coulombe, who gave me life. The first step began with them. When I came home from class one afternoon in the fourth grade and declared that I would become a writer, they never persuaded me to follow a different dream. Whether I thought I was Superman, a rock star, an astronaut, or a puppeteer; I'm sure stating that I was a writer was just as preposterous in their eyes, but they never showed that inclination and for that I am forever grateful. It was that love and support that helped me follow my dream. From them I learned to love the outdoors, thus helping me to realize that you can talk to God just by walking in his gardens – this was my first glimpse of religion. My creativity stems from their planted seed. It is because of them that I am the warm, caring individual that I am today – at least, that is what they might say if you asked them. However, I am just me: insecure and lost like so many.

I would like thank my surrogate family, Bob and Louise Bridges, and Ginny and Jeremy Miller, who let me be me at a rebellious time in my life. When I couldn't (or wouldn't) talk to my parents. In life we all adopt people who, with no questions asked, are honored to accept the title:

these four are mine. I owe them so much. If they only knew how much they have helped me grow.

My fourth grade teacher, Mrs. Hancock at R.F. Hazard Elementary School introduced me to the wonderful world of creative writing. To you they were simple assignments but to me they were what the fourth grade was all about. Creative writing time was MY time. Now if only you could see the monster you've created.

Michael Chuah, a friend I met on a retreat, who sat down and took five years' worth of expressed emotion and created a concept. You were able to understand and run with my ideas. You gave the book its first breath of life. The words took over after that. Thank you from the bottom of my heart.

Again, my best friend and soul sister Ginny Miller, who, through even my darkest moods (which are few in number depending on which one of us you ask), slaps me back into reality and keeps me on track. You have patiently waited on the sideline for this day. The footprints are still visible on my ass from your friendly little "nudges."

Armin Torrentos, Jr. Thank you for preserving the original concept of my book and making the second edition just as good as the original. Let this be the first of many projects together.

Regan Talley, an extraordinary force in her own right; we wrote our books together. You bounced ideas off of me and I bounced ideas off of you – what a team we make. Thank you for taking my author's picture. Now my big head is forever embossed on the back cover.

Virginia Blessing, my benefactor for this project.

Marcie Eanes, my editor and friend.

Damien Rangel, my endless ally and best friend.

And lastly, thank you to all those who hurt me along the way - - it was all of you who forced me to look inside of myself and face what was really there. Sometimes it was an ugly battle and you probably ran off just in time before there was any real carnage. This book is the souvenir from that trip. It's the journal of my heart.

Thank you.

Michael J. Coulombe

Narcissistic muses drenching with
            prophetic desire
chant in a hectic trance.
the poet breathes in the hypnotic tremors
                        (2/15/02)